A New Pet

First published in 2008
by Wayland

This paperback edition published in 2009

Text copyright © Claire Llewellyn 2008
Illustration copyright © Jacqueline East 2008

Wayland
338 Euston Road
London NW1 3BH

Wayland Australia
Hachette Children's Books
Level 17/207 Kent Street
Sydney, NSW 2000

Series editor: Louise John
Cover design: Paul Cherrill
Design: D.R.ink
Consultant: Shirley Bickler

A CIP catalogue record for this book is available from the British Library.

ISBN 9780750251792 (hbk)
ISBN 9780750251808 (pbk)

Printed in China

Wayland is a division of Hachette Children's Books,
an Hachette Livre UK Company

A New Pet

Written by Claire Llewellyn
Illustrated by Jacqueline East

WAYLAND

Dad took Pip to the pet shop on Saturday. Pip wanted to find a new pet.

Pip looked at a rabbit.
"Rabbits are good pets,"
said Dad.
"I don't like rabbits much,"
said Pip.

Then Pip looked at a fish
but the fish didn't look
at him.

"I don't like fish much,"
said Pip.

"Look at that dog,"
said Pip.

The dog jumped up.
"Get down!" said Pip.

11

Then Pip looked at a rat.
The rat was very smelly.

"I don't like rats much,"
said Pip.

"Dad, look at this snake!"
said Pip.
"Sssss!" hissed the snake
and it stuck out its tongue.

Pip looked at a fluffy cat.

"Cats are good pets,"
said Pip. But this cat
didn't want to play.

"Ark! Ark!" called a parrot
in a cage.
"I don't like parrots
much," said Pip.

19

Then Pip looked at a
hamster.

The hamster looked at Pip.

"Can he be my new pet,
Dad?" said Pip.

Pip liked his new pet.
"I'm going to call him
Henry," he said.

Then Pip and Dad took
Henry the hamster home.

START READING is a series of highly enjoyable books for beginner readers. They have been carefully graded to match the Book Bands widely used in schools. This enables readers to be sure they choose books that match their own reading ability.

The Bands are:

Pink / Band 1
Red / Band 2
Yellow / Band 3
Blue / Band 4
Green / Band 5
Orange / Band 6
Turquoise / Band 7
Purple / Band 8
Gold / Band 9

START READING books can be read independently or shared with an adult. They promote the enjoyment of reading through satisfying stories supported by fun illustrations.

Claire Llewellyn has written many books for children. Some of them are about real things like animals or the Moon. Others are storybooks, like this one. Claire has two children of her own, but they are getting too big for stories like this. She hopes that you will enjoy reading her stories instead now!

Jacqueline East scratched her first drawing into her mum's sideboard when she was six! She has enjoyed drawing animals ever since and has a naughty dog called Scampi, who often appears in her books! When Jacqueline is not drawing, she likes to dance and play the guitar.